For Kevin -L.B.

For Mum and Dad, my inspiration -S.W.

BLOOMSBURY
CHILDREN'S
BOOKS

First published in Great Britain in 2000 by Bloomsbury Publishing Plc
38 Soho Square, London W1V 5DF

Text copyright © Lisa Bruce 2000
Illustrations copyright © Stephen Waterhouse 2000
The moral right of the author and illustrator has been asserted.

A CIP catalogue record for this book is available from the British Library.
ISBN 0 7475 4763 7

Designed by Dawn Apperley

Printed and bound by South China Printing Co.

1 3 5 7 9 10 8 6 4 2

Engines, Engines

Lisa Bruce and Stephen Waterhouse

BLOOMSBURY
CHILDREN'S
BOOKS

Have you ever been on a journey?
Riding on a train can be such fun.
There are lots of new and exciting things
to see. So step aboard the number engines
and let's travel together through the
far away land of India...

Engine, engine number ONE

Setting off in the midday sun

Engine, engine number TWO

Past the temple of Vishnu

Engine, engine number THREE

Women wearing bright sari

Engine, engine number FOUR

Chugging along the desert floor

Engine, engine number FIVE

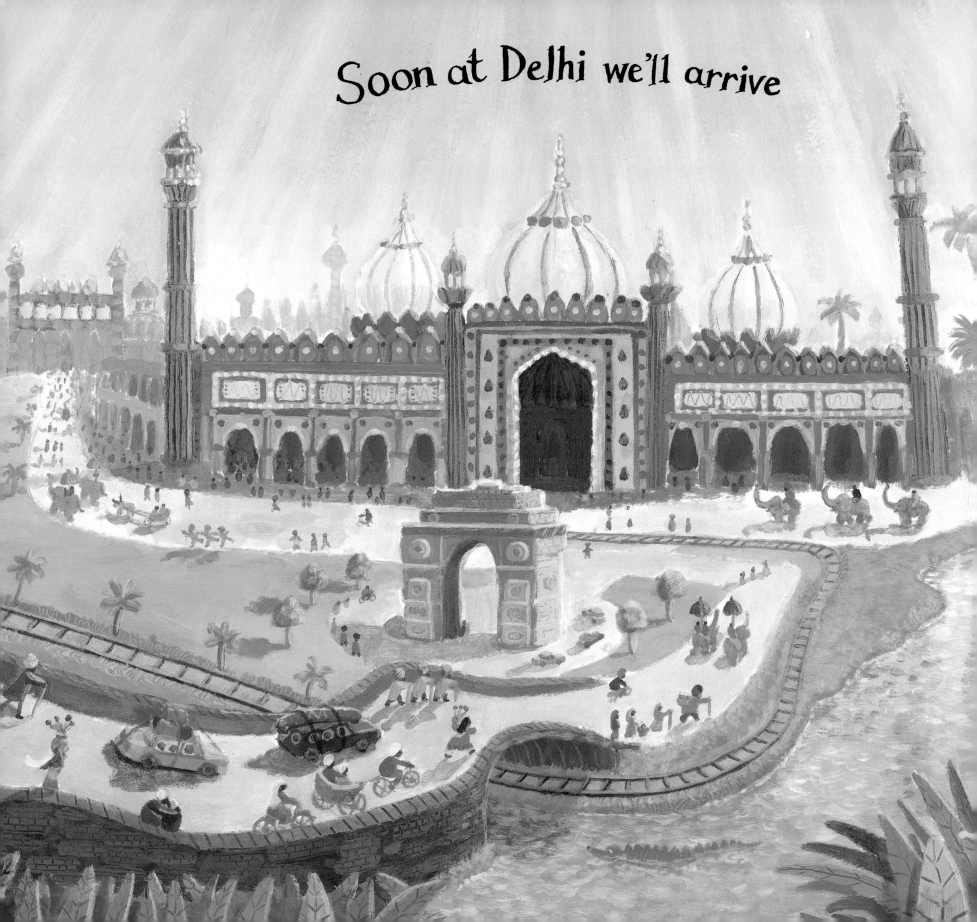

Soon at Delhi we'll arrive

Engine, engine number SIX

Naughty monkeys playing tricks

Engine, engine number SEVEN

The Himalayas reach up to heaven

Engine, engine number EIGHT

Past the palace with the golden gate

Engine, engine number NINE

Steaming down the Bombay line

Engine, engine number TEN

Follow the Ganges home again

The journey's finished, our fun is done

To travel again, go back to ONE!